The Three Little Pigs

First Aladdin Paperbacks Edition September 1998

Aladdin Paperbacks
An imprint of Simon & Schuster Children's Publishing Division
1230 Avenue of the Americas
New York, NY 10020

READY-TO-READ is a registered trademark of Simon & Schuster, Inc.
Also available in a Simon & Schuster Books for Young Readers Edition.
The text for this book was set in Utopia.
Printed and bound in the United States of America
10 9 8 7 6 5 4 3 2

The Library of Congress has cataloged the Simon & Schuster Books for
Young Readers edition as follows:

Miles, Betty.
The three little pigs / by Betty Miles ; illustrated by Paul Meisel.
p.   cm. — (Ready-to-read)
Summary: The familiar story of three pigs who outsmart a wolf is retold
primarily using dialogue.
ISBN 0-689-81788-6 (hc)
[1. Folklore.] I. Meisel, Paul, ill. II. Three little pigs. English. III. Title.
IV. Series.
PZ8.1.M4955Th 1998
398.24'529633—dc21
[E]   97-16007
CIP   AC
ISBN 0-689-81789-4 (pbk)

The Three Little Pigs

Written by
Betty Miles

Illustrated by
Paul Meisel

Ready-to-Read
Aladdin Paperbacks

OLD STORIES FOR NEW READERS

The Three Little Pigs is an old story, and old stories are good for new readers. When they know what is going to happen, it's easier to read the words that tell about it.

Old stories often use the same words, like "Little Pig, Little Pig, let me come in" over and over again. A new reader begins to expect those words, to enjoy them, and to learn them.

And rhyming words help new readers. The words in this story, like "huff" and puff," are fun to say and easy to read.

You give your new reader a good start when you read out loud to each other. In this book, all the words are the animals' talk. Your child can read one animal's words and you can read another's.

Take time to enjoy the story and the pictures. You can help your reader by talking about what is happening on the page and what might happen next. You can point to familiar words in the pictures. You can point to words that rhyme, and you can help by asking what sound a word begins with.

Most of all, you can help by reading together often. Your new reader can read with you or with a grandparent, a babysitter, an older brother, sister, or a friend. New readers love to share their books!

Hello, Little Pig.
What are you doing?

I am making a house!
I am making it with straw.
See? Straw makes
a good, safe house.

Ha, ha, ha, Little Pig!
You will see
a straw house
is not safe
from me!

Go away, Wolf!
I am going inside.

And I am going to get you!

Little Pig, Little Pig,
let me come in!

Knock, knock!
Knock, knock, knock!

Not by the hair
of my chinny-chin-chin!

Then I'll huff
and I'll puff
and I'll blow your house in!

Huff! Puff! BLOW!

Help!

Help!
Wolf is coming!
Let me help you
make your house!

Hello, Little Pigs.
What are you doing?

We are making a house.
We are making it with sticks.
See? Sticks make
a good, safe house.

13

Ha, ha, ha, Little Pigs!

You will see
a stick house
is not safe from me!

Go away, Wolf!
We are going inside.

And I am going to get you!

Little Pigs, Little Pigs,
let me come in!

Knock, knock!
Knock, knock, knock!

Not by the hair
of my
chinny-chin-chin!

Not by the hair
of *my* chinny-chin-chin!

Then I'll huff
and I'll puff
and I'll blow your house in!

Huff! Puff! BLOW!

Help! Help!

Help!
Wolf is coming!
Let us help you
make your house!

19

Hello, Little Pigs.
What are you doing?

We are making
a house!
We are
making it
with bricks.
Bricks make
a good, safe house.

20

Ha, ha, ha!
You will see
a brick house
is not safe
from me!

Go away, Wolf!
We are going inside.

And I am going to get you!

Little Pigs, Little Pigs,
let me come in!

Knock, knock!
Knock, knock, knock!

Not by the hair
of my chinny-chin-chin!

Not by the hair
of my
chinny-chin-chin!

And not by the hair
of *my* chinny-chin-chin!

Then I'll huff
and I'll puff
and I'll blow
your house in!

Huff, Puff!
Huff, Puff!

**Huff, Puff, Huff, Puff—
BLOW!**

Ha, ha, ha, Wolf!
Bricks make
a good, safe house!

Little Pigs, Little Pigs,
Let me come in!

**Knock, knock,
Knock, knock, knock!**

NO!
Go away, Wolf.
We are making soup!

I love soup!
Please let me in!

PIG

I'm coming in!

29

OWWWWW!

Goodbye, Pigs!

Goodbye, Wolf!

Bricks make a
good, safe house!
And we are
safe inside.

Mmm! Good soup!

THE END